I Want a Trumpet!

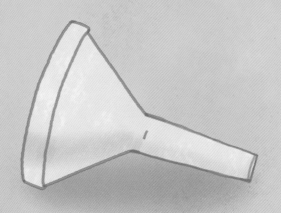

Licensed by The Illuminated Film Company
Based on the LITTLE PRINCESS animation series © The Illuminated Film Company 2007
Made under licence by Andersen Press Ltd., London
'I Want a Trumpet!' episode written by Dan Wicksman.
Producer Iain Harvey. Director Edward Foster.
© The Illuminated Film Company/Tony Ross 2007
Design and layout © Andersen Press Ltd., 2007.
Printed and bound in China by C&C Offset Printing.
10 9 8 7 6 5 4 3 2 1
British Library Cataloguing in Publication Data available.

ISBN: 978 1 84270 708 1 (Trade edition)
ISBN: 978 1 84939 701 8 (Riverside Books edition)

I Want a Trumpet!

Tony Ross

Andersen Press · London

It was a peaceful day in the castle garden, until a cheeky crow swooped down onto the royal vegetable patch.

"Hey!" shouted the Gardener.

"Get away from my carrots!"

Inside the Little Princess had other things
on her mind. She had found a
mysterious brown box.
"What's that?" she asked the Maid.
The Maid picked the parcel up.
"That is for the King."

The Little Princess followed the Maid into the dining room.

"Oh, splendid," cried the King. "It's arrived!"

"But what is it?" asked the Little Princess.

The King started unwrapping the parcel. "I'll show you."

Inside was a square, painted box with a handle.
The King gave the handle a good wind, then stood back.

"Oh!" cried the Little Princess.
Suddenly the box sprang open and a tiny
clockwork figure with a trumpet popped up.

The little trumpeter began to dance and play along
to the King's music box.
"Ahh!" marvelled the King, closing his eyes.

"Can I play the trumpet too, Dad?" asked the
Little Princess.
The King wasn't listening.
The Little Princess tried something else. "Can I have
ice cream for breakfast?"
"Whatever you say, poppet," mumbled the King.

The Little Princess went downstairs to sulk on her potty.
"That music-thing makes him go all silly," she frowned.
Suddenly the Little Princess got up. "I need to find a trumpet!"

"No, no, no…" murmured the Little Princess, rummaging through her toy box. "There must be a trumpet somewhere." She made up her mind to try the garden.

"Gardener!" called the Little Princess. "Do you have a trumpet in your toolbox?"

"Hello, Little Princess!" smiled the Gardener. He put down the scarecrow he was making and scratched his head.

"Er, no I haven't."

"Come on, Gilbert," sighed the Little Princess. "Let's go back indoors."

"Geroff!" cried the Gardener, spotting another crow.

"Oh dearie me."

The Little Princess tried the kitchen next.

"Do you have a trumpet?"

"*La musique?*" bellowed the Chef. "Can't you see I am very busy?"

The Little Princess hunted through the cupboards herself.

Finally she pulled out an object that looked just the right shape.

"A trumpet!"

she squealed, getting ready to play.

"Ah *non!*" shouted the Chef.

"Shoo from my kitchen!"

Up in her bedroom, the Little Princess huffed and puffed into her new trumpet. Nothing happened.

"There's something stuck inside it," she realised.

The Little Princess blew her biggest blow ever. A dried pea shot out of the end. Now she could play properly.

HONNNNNNKKK!
"Lovely!"
giggled the Little Princess.
"I'm going to play it to Daddy."

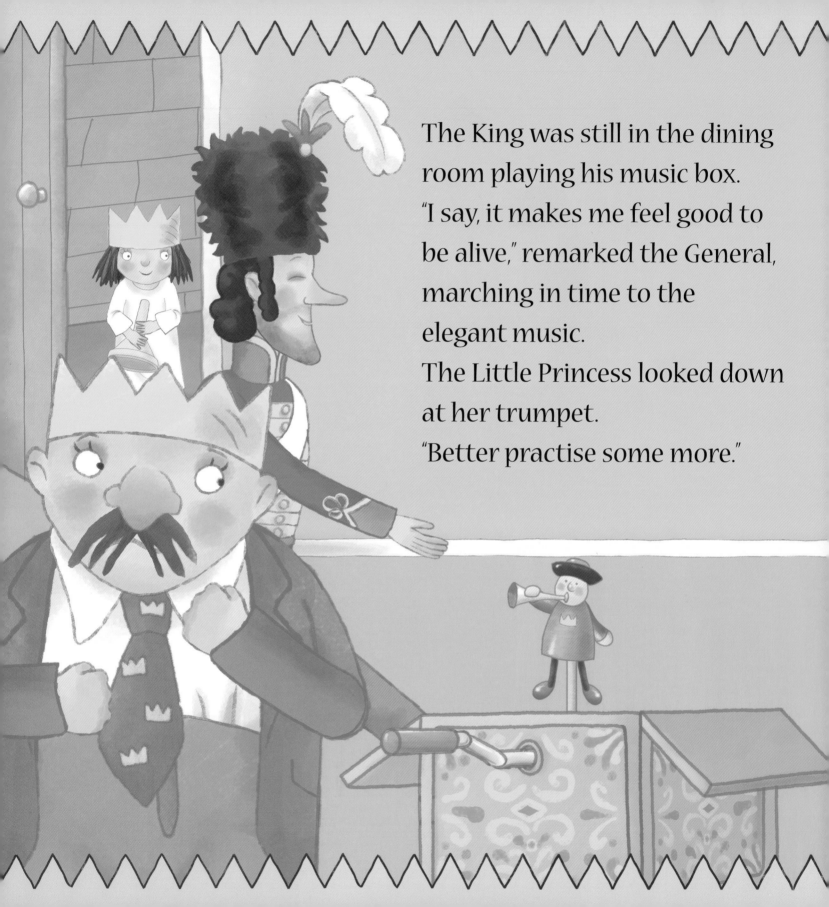

The King was still in the dining room playing his music box.
"I say, it makes me feel good to be alive," remarked the General, marching in time to the elegant music.
The Little Princess looked down at her trumpet.
"Better practise some more."

"Goodness!"
gasped the King all of a sudden.
A spring had snapped in the
music box, stopping the little
trumpeter's tune.

In a quiet castle corridor, the Little Princess took a deep breath. She didn't see the Queen step round the corner.

HONNNNNNNNNNNKKK!

"Aaagggh!" screamed the Queen.

The ice cream cone she'd been enjoying sailed through the air…
straight into a royal portrait.
"I think I'll practise somewhere else," said the Little Princess helpfully.

The Little Princess found a cosy
place to practise under the
kitchen table.

HONNNKKKKKKK!

"Ah *non!*" shrieked the Chef,
lurching forward to save his jelly.
It was time to move on.

"Do you like music?" asked
the Little Princess,
giving the Maid a fright.

The Maid backed out of the laundry room.
"I like it when I hear it."

The Little Princess proudly burst into the dining room.

"Do you want to hear my trumpet?"

"Not now, poppet," said the King, barely looking over his shoulder. "We're taking the music box out for the Gardener to fix."
"I do hope he can!" whispered the General. The Little Princess tiptoed sadly out of the room.

The Little Princess ran outside. "Nobody likes my trumpet."
In the distance, she could hear voices. The Gardener must have
fixed the music box! The King had set it up on a tub
by the vegetable patch.

"I feel bad," said the Little Princess, climbing a tree for a better look. She could see the Gardener tightening a screw on the side of the box.

"That should do it," he announced. The music box tinkled into life.

"I know!" cried the Little Princess. "The Gardener hasn't heard my trumpet!"

She grabbed Gilbert and ran over to the vegetable patch.

The Gardener didn't notice the Little Princess – he was having more trouble with crows again.

HONNNKKKKKK!

The crows squawked in surprise and fluttered away.

"What a marvellous noise," chuckled the Gardener. "Well done!"

"I'm going to try it on Daddy now," grinned the Little Princess.

The King looked up in dismay.
A naughty crow had stolen his
toy trumpeter.
"Release him, you scoundrel!" cried
the General.
HONNNKKKKKKK!

The startled crow dropped the puppet and flapped away. The King caught the trumpeter then turned round to see where the noise had come from.

The Little Princess beamed up at him.

"Well done, poppet!" said the King. "We want you to play lots and lots…"

"...especially in the vegetable garden!" added the Gardener.